written by
Meg Fleming

illustrated by
Sarah Jane Wright

I HEART YOU

BEACH LANE BOOKS • New York   London   Toronto   Sydney   New Delhi

For Laura, Andy, and Ben, who fill my heart,
and for Kevin, who holds it—M. F.

To Kenneth, Addie, Ian, Ella, and Anders,
with all my heart—S. J. W.

BEACH LANE BOOKS • An imprint of Simon & Schuster Children's Publishing Division
• 1230 Avenue of the Americas, New York, New York 10020 • Text copyright © 2016 by Megan Lentz •
Illustrations copyright © 2016 by Sarah Jane Wright • All rights reserved, including the right of reproduction
in whole or in part in any form. • BEACH LANE BOOKS is a trademark of Simon & Schuster, Inc. • For information
about special discounts for bulk purchases, please contact Simon & Schuster Special Sales at 1-866-506-1949 or
business@simonandschuster.com. • The Simon & Schuster Speakers Bureau can bring authors to your live event. For more
information or to book an event, contact the Simon & Schuster Speakers Bureau at 1-866-248-3049 or visit our website
at www.simonspeakers.com. • Book design by Lauren Rille • The text for this book was set in Personal Manifesto. • The illustrations for
this book were rendered pencil and gouache. • Manufactured in China • 0916 SCP • First Edition • Library of Congress Cataloging-in-Publication
Data • Names: Fleming, Meg. | Wright, Sarah Jane, illustrator. • Title: I heart you / Meg Fleming ; illustrated by Sarah Jane Wright. • Other titles: I love you •
Description: First edition. | New York : Beach Lane Books, [2016] | Summary: "A rhyming picture book about the loving parent-child relationship in animal and
human families"—Provided by publisher. • Identifiers: LCCN 2015022831 | ISBN 978-1-4424-8895-3 (hardcover : alk. paper) | ISBN 978-1-4424-8887-8
(eBook) • Subjects: | CYAC: Stories in rhyme. | Parent and child—Fiction. | Parental behavior in animals—Fiction. | Love—Fiction. | Animals—Fiction. • Classification:
LCC PZ8.3.F639 Iah 2016 | DDC [E]—dc21 LC record available at http://lccn.loc.gov/2015022831 • 10 9 8 7 6 5 4 3 2 1

I see you.

I miss you.

I hug you.

I kiss you.

I hide you.

I tease you.

I find you.

I squeeze you.

I chase you.

I slow you.

I lift you.

I grow you.

I swim you.

I hop you.

I start you.

I stop you.

I sway you.

I swing you.

I snug you.

I sing you.

I hear you.

I let you.

I know you.

I get you.

I pull you.

I tug you.

I hold you.

I love you.